MUSINGS OF A SERPENT
A Collection of Short Stories, Poems, and Writings

MUSINGS OF A SERPENT

A Collection of Short Stories, Poems, and Writings

Book 1

Nicole Rivera

Isaiah Publications (New York City)
cs@isaiahpublications.com

For additional titles by Nicole Rivera, please visit http://www.nicolerivera.com.

To my lovable, independent serpent, Dumpling. You are a master storyteller.

CONTENTS

INTRODUCTION

Musings of a Serpent is a cocreation between myself and Dumpling, to whom I am a guardian. She is a brilliant-orange snake with the demeanor and elegance of a queen. She is incredibly self-aware and knows explicitly what she wants at all times. She has an enormous and formidable personality but is also gentle and understanding. To some she is just a snake; to me she is an expression of a greater source that has come to seek joy and freedom and to be, quite simply, a snake.

Snakes are often thought of as a sinister lot and are feared by a large part of humanity. They can evoke both feelings of enthrallment and repulsion. Their reputation as evil is undeserved. In fact, snakes are elegant, majestic creatures. In the mythology of many cultures, snakes are depicted as a symbol of fertility, birth, and creation, as well as transformation and renewal, as in the shedding of their skin. In ancient Egypt the cobra represents wisdom.

I began writing with Dumpling out of sheer pleasure. You see, Dumpling enjoys when I tell her stories. One day, I began, as usual, to tell her a story, which became *The Jewel of Prague*. Afterward, I had the urgent desire to write it down. I enjoyed it so much that I decided to write down more of the stories I told instead of just telling them, but this time I wanted her to tell me the stories. Thus, we have the collection at hand.

I am sure by now you are wondering how it is possible for a snake to tell a story or for me to even hear it. The art of communicating with species other than our own is far from new. Many individuals speak with their pets and wild animals every day. Indeed, our ancient ancestors lived close to the land and its inhabitants and were in tune with their surroundings. The native peoples across continents respected and appreciated the animals and plants, coexisting with them in harmony and were able to commune with them on a deeper level of knowing. We, as a species, have the innate ability to communicate with all that surrounds us. Unfortunately, over time, we have lost this skill. It is simply a matter of being quiet and relaxed and allowing yourself to receive the thoughts, images, and feelings that are being projected to you from the other. Everyone is unique, and so each individual will have their own way of receiving.

In *Musings of a Serpent*, Dumpling tells stories of her majesty, her beauty, and the important and inspiring qualities of her species, as well as lighthearted stories that show her playful side. She shares her fantasies and desires and shows a reflective, caring side of herself, as seen in the poem *Alone*. She also depicts her species as divine beings that warrant our respect and that provide a benefit to humanity. In some cases, you will be privy to her own personal thoughts and feelings, as in the writing *The Pearl*.

Our sole intention in writing this collection was to experience the joy of writing together. Every morning I began by asking Dumpling, "What story do you want to tell today?" I listened and Dumpling spoke, and together we created the following. I never knew what was going to be written beforehand. The stories flowed effortlessly and the endings were always a surprise. It was a learning process for me, and for Dumpling it was exciting to be able to express herself in a fun and unique way. She also says that it's nice to be heard.

It is our hope that the stories presented in this book will encourage you to see the nobility and beauty of snakes as we do and to spread the good word about their species.

THE JEWEL OF PRAGUE

Once there was a lovely, slender, formidable serpent. Her skin was radiant and silky and a brilliant-orange color, with black glimmering diamonds cascading down the length of her back. She called her home the picturesque streets of Prague, where she could be found slithering among the people with her lean, strong neck erect and proud, flicking her tongue, sensing the beauty of the air and the essence of its people, for in this land she was not feared but instead revered and feverishly sought after. When caught in one's sight, she was considered a blessing to them, to their families, and to their country as a whole. The economy was sure to rise, the people were sure to prosper in love, happiness, and wealth, and the animals were sure to continue to live their lives free and in peace.

To the people, she was lovingly known as the Jewel of Prague, and as she slithered through the streets with such honor, the people bowed to her and smiled. Some tipped their hats while others curtsied. Some were so impassioned at the sight of her that they scurried about the village shouting gleefully, "I lay my eyes upon the Jewel! I lay my eyes upon the Jewel!"

But there was more to the Jewel than mere beauty and foretelling for her people. The villagers did not go mad for these gains alone; instead, they were delirious with joy, for they knew that if one was chosen by the Jewel to experience a more intimate encounter as a gift from her, one was given the honor of asking a question of her. Why, you ask, was this privilege so sought after by the villagers? It must be because of her uncanny ability to speak the truth, and in speaking the truth, her answer most assuredly came true.

So you can imagine how honored and utterly thrilled an unsuspecting villager was when the Jewel began her ascent up his leg, around his waist, and round his chest. He stood quite still and in a quiver, when at last she rested at the peak of his head. She observed the wonders of the world and relished in his point of view.

The villager breathed a deep breath and formulated his question. He cleared his throat, collected his thoughts, and asked nervously, "Oh, my dear, honorable Jewel of Prague, will I prosper at my business? Will peace be bestowed upon me and my family?"

The Jewel flicked her tongue. She slid around the middle of the villager's head, gripped him tightly, and stared him in the eye. The villager unwillingly closed his eyes, for the power of the serpent commanded it to be so. It was in the darkness of the villager's mind that he heard the serpent reply, "Yes, with perseverance and focus, you will prosper, and peace will be yours. I am sure of this to be true."

And the villager, with eyes still firmly shut, wept a thousand tears and gave a thousand thanks and said, "My honorable Jewel, what can I possibly offer you in return for such a profitable prediction?"

The serpent replied, "Promise me that you will do as I have commanded, thus fulfilling your desire. This is all I ask."

The villager agreed wholeheartedly, and upon opening his eyes, the Jewel disappeared, leaving a sparkle in her wake. The villager jumped for joy, flailing his arms in the air, proclaiming, "I have been blessed by the Jewel! I have been blessed by the Jewel!" and dashed home as fast as his plump little legs could carry him. There, he reported his good fortune to his wife and children, and they too leapt for joy.

The serpent continued on through the streets of Prague and ultimately returned to the peace and tranquility of the marvelous countryside. She swerved her way through the grass and up the bark of an old friend, where she basked in the sun on a sturdy branch, enjoying the beauty of the sky. As the Jewel of Prague relaxed in the glory of the world, she rejuvenated for herself and her people.

True Reflections

I've never seen a mirror,
A reflection, some would say.
Indeed, I sense through others
My presence, my sultry way.

I gather from these humans;
I am quite distinct,
For there are those who dash in fear,
While others stop and think.

There are those that will cringe,
Those that choose to hurt,
Those that are curious,
And those I leave inert.

But then there is this one
Who I see every day.
I know her as my companion.
She looks at me in this way:

She stares at me with wonder,
Frozen in a trance,
Smiling happily,
Joyful in her dance.

She fancies me quite beautiful,
Radiant, alluring,
Independent, formidable,
And rather adoring.

She admires me,
Appreciates me,
Fawns over me,
In awe of me.

She kisses me with passion
And speaks to me in words.
Though I do not understand,
Her song is like a bird.

And when she grips me in her arms,
She embraces me so tight.
I'd rather slither away,
But I hesitate; she's so bright.

I relish this tenderness
I've never known before.
Warm against her chest,
I savor it all the more.

I appreciate her eternally.
I cherish our connection.
Of this I am quite sure:
She is my true reflection.

Message in the Sands

The sands of time wait for no one,
Nor do they stop when I am gone,
So I crawl about merrily,
Creating my own song.

"What shall I create?" I ponder. And then, as if an unknown force heard my cries, I concede to the power of the wind.

I swerve and then curve
Around, slightly down.

Up I go,
Then round the bend,
To repeat the same
All over again
Until I meet the beginning, thus, the end.

I bask.

A vibration from above has me in a wonder.
It trembles beneath me like a wild thunder.

I glance up.
It twirls its wings,
Lands on the sand, serene.

A human appears from the belly of the beast.

It walks toward me, glares at me, wonders about me.
Two round circles dress its eyes.
It fusses with them, grabs hold of them, straightens
them, puts them back on again.

It follows my swerves and curves,
My rounds, then downs.
I stare when I should crawl away
But curiosity begs me to stay.

Crouched down, head like a spear, eyes like a hawk, it
traces my lines step by step. Perplexed bewilderment
upon its face, it wept.

Enthusiastically, it swivels its hand upon an object it
held.
What it was I could not tell.

It contemplates the swerves, then the curves, continues
to excitedly twirl its hand.

Hesitantly, it walks toward me,
Squints at me,
Till it is uncomfortably near to me, and says, "Excuse
me, my dear serpent; I am in somewhat of a daze. I saw
this message from above and was compelled to descend
upon it. I must ask of you, who created such wonder-
ment in the sand?"

I said, "Why, it was I, with the help of the wind."

And it laughed, and it chuckled,
Held onto its buckle.
It bent over in glee
And fell to its knees and exclaimed, "You magnificent creature!"

"Thank you," I said, "but I merely followed my heart."
In amazement, the human scurried about for its object.
It held it up with a smile upon its face and revealed to me what was, most assuredly, a heart.

The Queen

There once lived a queen of very slender and sleek proportions; her eyes as black as the darkness of the deep sea, her skin of pure silk with a sheen so bright it blinded those who dared gaze upon her. For you see, only those pure of heart and mind could lay their eyes upon the queen without being blinded. If they did not carry purity within their hearts, their sight was stricken from them for eternity. They were cast out of her kingdom; sent to work the mines. All day and all night, they shoveled the coals that kept the queen's throne warm from beneath the earth. They remained hard at work until they attained clarity—none ever did.

Very few dared gaze upon the queen, and those who chose to tempt their fate did so for one reason: immortality. To be able to look upon the queen in her true nature was to be filled with appreciation of all life, to have clarity, inner peace, and understanding of the world, to be able to walk among humanity and not be swayed here nor there but to remain pure in knowing. This was extremely rare. Nevertheless, there were those who dared.

First, there was a man who displayed brute force. He was muscular yet agile. He came before the queen with gladness in his heart, for he had conquered the body. He was strong yet he knelt before the queen in agony as her light shone upon him. He was blinded and cast out to work the mines.

Second, there was a woman who displayed a

gentle nature. She came before the queen with gladness in her heart, for she had sacrificed herself continuously for her fellow humans. She was kindhearted, yet she too knelt before the queen in despair as her light shined upon her. She was blinded and cast out to work the mines.

Third, there was a child who displayed playfulness. The child, sent before the queen by its parents, was lighthearted and filled with laughter, yet it too knelt in anguish at the rays of the queen and was banished to work the mines, for it carried the deep scars of its parents and the adults who surrounded it.

Fourth, there was a wee little mouse who displayed strength, kindheartedness, playfulness, curiosity, cleverness, and joy. The queen shone herself on the mouse, and it stood still. "You are the most beautiful I have ever seen," it said.

The queen replied, "Do you realize what I am?"

"Yes," said the mouse. "You're a serpent."

"Why do you not run from me? I am made to eat you. Do you not know this?"

"Yes, I am aware of this, but I am not afraid. I understand and honor our roles in this world. I know that I must go about my life with gladness in my heart, no matter of your existence."

"Quite true, quite true," said the queen. "Pray, do go on."

"Many see me as just a mouse, but I know I am so much more. My dear queen, I respect you, and I respect myself. I came before you to give my life to you so that I might experience a new life."

Upon pondering the heartfelt utterances of the sage mouse, the queen slithered with joy, for there was, at last, a soul who was worthy of immortality; be it a human, a plant, or an animal in the form of a wee little mouse, it did not matter. The queen said, "You have earned your immortality. You shall live forever."

The mouse eagerly raced toward the queen and but for a brief moment, there was silence. With the utmost respect and appreciation for the mouse, the queen flicked her tongue and said, "Good."

Transformations

One dark, starry night, there lay, hidden within the depths of the forest, an animal of a curious nature. This animal was deep in thought, and as this animal thought, it decided it wanted to experience itself as a different species. Although it was honored to be a part of a species that has survived on earth for millions of years, it had concluded that it knew everything it wanted to know about being a serpent.

But how, it thought, can I go about accomplishing such a tremendous feat as transformation?

It decided that it would travel. It did not know where it was headed nor where it would ultimately arrive, but it felt that if it remained in the same place, it would never experience the change that it sought, so it crawled off in pursuit of its desire.

It crept through the night; it wriggled over mountains, squirmed up trees, wandered beyond hills, and glided through the waters. And as it slithered through the waters, something in the distance caught its eye. It was white and glowed like the sun. As it neared this glimmering wonder that lay at the bottom of the ocean, it opened wide, like a clam. The voice from within the wonder beckoned the animal nearer and nearer till it leaped out of the sands and snatched the animal up. It shut its jaw tight.

The walls of the wonder were iridescent and shimmered. Its rays pulsated and spoke. "I have heard through the waves of the ocean that you wish to take the form of another?"

The animal answered, "Yes, I want to experience being another species. I want to begin anew."

"What species do you wish to be?" said the wonder.

"I am not quite sure," replied the animal.

The wonder proceeded to offer to the animal different forms to wear. First, was the form of a lion. The animal squeezed its way through the paw of the lion and began to roar. It hunted with the pride, stalked its prey, and fed on zebra. Licking its lips, it said, "I'd like to try another."

The wonder proceeded to offer the animal the form of a whale. The animal slid through the tip of the fin of the whale and began to groan and snort, calling out to the others in its group. It migrated with the pod, hunted, and fed. It slapped its mighty tail against the waters and said, "I'd like to try another."

The wonder proceeded to offer the animal the form of an eagle. The animal swerved its way through the beak of the eagle and began to soar high into the sky. It flapped its wings harder and harder and glided among the clouds. It relished in the breeze that brushed up against its feathers. It delighted in the speed at which it was able to arrive at one place from another. It reveled in the ease with which it was able to traverse the land, no boundaries or obstacles to overcome and said, "I have found my new species. I am free."

The Unsuspecting Ballerina

There once was a petite young lady, oh, of about nineteen years of age, who desired, from the depths of her heart, to dance with grace and elegance akin to the accomplished artists of her day. Regrettably, she was a clumsy young lass with two left feet, though she always tried, with the utmost care and attention to detail, to glide seamlessly upon the ballet dance floor like the others, who her teacher lovingly referred to as swans.

"That'll do," the teacher would say, shrugging her off, interrupting her practice performance. Bowing her head in disgrace, the young lady would leave the spotlight to sit on the sidelines.

On her way home one evening, she stopped in a nearby park. Defeated, she plopped herself upon an ancient rock under a majestic oak tree that spread its branches wide. She felt protected under its umbrella and proceeded to cry in despair, for her dream of becoming a successful ballerina was slowly deteriorating.

As she wept, she heard through her tears a sensuous, sly voice say, "Do not fret. I will teach you the art of dance."

"Who's there?" she cried, as it was too dark for her to see.

"It is I."

And upon these words, she turned around, and there before her eyes was a long, willowy serpent coiled around a thick branch, glaring at her with its deep,

21

black eyes, which permeated her very soul. It wore the color of twilight, with glistening white stars dressing the whole of its body. Startled, she jumped back with her hand to her heart.

"Why, you are a serpent. How can you teach me to dance?"

"If you will allow me to slither upon you, your question will most assuredly be answered." The young lady acquiesced, and the serpent slid its way upon her shoulder and softly around her neck. She twitched and whispered, "Oh my." Without notice, she was thrust to her feet and began to move ever so smoothly and alluringly. "What is happening?" she said, having no control of her body.

"Do not think; feel. Be easy and allow yourself to be swept away by my song."

As the serpent slithered its way around her chest, down and about her waist, twisting itself around her leg, ascending once again, overwhelming her body in the most hypnotic and silkiest of ways, the young lady began to respond to its touch and swayed along with it, absorbing the essence and beauty of the serpent. No longer was she the bumbling ballerina with two left feet. Instead, she was the most graceful, elegant, and sensual ballerina that one could ever lay eyes upon. Every slither, every slink, every twirl of its tail, every swerve of its neck, every slow gesticulation, every curve of its body stimulated hers. She danced as no one has ever danced before.

Unbeknownst to the serpent or the young lady,

a crowd, mesmerized by the sultry, peaceful movements of the couple, had gathered around. They gazed upon the two as they flowed with the wind, gliding about in a trance to an inner music that could only have mirrored that of a gentle, classical nature.

At the request of the most renowned performance arena in the world, the serpent and the young lady later performed in front of a full house, from which they received an enormous amount of praise. From there, the young lady went on to fulfill her dream as the most sought-after ballerina, and the serpent returned to the majestic oak tree.

Language of the Gods

There once was a serpent that was known across the whole of the earth. It traveled far and wide, across the stormy seas and through the countless lands. Everywhere it crawled, regardless of whom or what it encountered, it had the uncanny ability to communicate with all who crossed its path,

From the trees and the plants,
The birds and the bees,
The lions and the bears,
And the creatures of the sea.

It even had the ability to communicate with humans

From America to Brazil,
Russia, and Europe;
From Asia to Africa,
Wherever it showed up.

How, you ask, was this prodigy of a serpent able to communicate with everyone and everything? I'm not quite sure, but together we will find out. I have traveled my whole life in search of this elusive serpent in the hopes that I might communicate with it and ask it of its gift.

Let's begin with what we know. The existence of this rare serpent and its unfathomable abilities has been well documented on monuments and cave walls and in shrines, temples, and churches, on certain stones of great significance, and even in the heavens. All of these ancient relics and petroglyphs tell us that this particular serpent embodied the greatest speech of all—the language of the Gods. No one knows how it managed to obtain such brilliance. Suffice it to say that it is exceptional indeed and has been revered throughout the ages. Humans have painted it, carved it, written about it, and told stories about it that have been passed down from generation to generation. The animals and forests of the world have, no doubt, cherished this serpent in their own ways, most assuredly in their minds.

There are many specific encounters the serpent has had with the people of this world. One tribe on the coast of Africa painted an image on a wall of the serpent whispering in the ear of the chief hunter. Was it advising the hunter on where to hunt? The image revealed the answer to be yes, for the artist had drawn a brilliant sun that lit up the area of the land where the animals hid, but not only did the light shone on the animals as a whole, it seemed to be explicitly lit over an animal who the serpent must have known was ready for its transition, for the animal that was targeted was drawn with a huge smile as if to say, "Choose me."

In a small town in the country of Argentina, a monstrous stone carving of the serpent is set prominently within the town circle. The serpent's mouth is open wide, with its tongue sticking out. Within its belly is carved a human lying down, seemingly asleep. Above the human is an illustration of what could be interpreted as a fortuitous event, for it portrayed happiness being bestowed upon a family. Smiles were strewn across all the people's faces as they jumped with cheerfulness. It would appear that the human recorded the vision it had during sleep. Did it see the serpent in its waking life as well, or did the serpent appear in its sleeping life because the human could not receive its communication while conscious? I wonder.

Among the remnants of an Indian tribe in the Americas, near the Mississippi, I happened upon some interesting art that was carved into several rocks. This particular tribe depicted the serpent casting a ray of light directly toward the middle of the forehead of a tribesman, as if it were beaming it a signal, a message of sorts.

In Russia, Asia, and India, the depictions were quite similar. The serpent was continuously illustrated wrapped around the head of the chief, which would seem to signify that the proper use of the mind played a key role in the process of communication. Then I questioned, Was it primarily the honor only of chiefs to communicate with the serpent because only they had the wisdom to receive the communication, or did everyone have the ability to communicate?

I have traveled endlessly and with great resolve. I am a bit exhausted. As I continued my journey through the Americas, eager to stumble upon this curiosity of a serpent, I stopped for a moment in repose beneath a lustrous olden tree. I rested my backpack on a nearby rock and closed my eyes, when suddenly I felt something smooth and silky crisscross my legs. I opened my eyes in disbelief and in wonder, for there in front of me was my treasure: the ingenious serpent. I unmistakably recognized it from the ancient arts. It was slender and moved elegantly. It was a deep crimson red, with diamonds along its slinky back. It raised its head to meet me eye to eye. It flicked its tongue. I breathed a deep sigh, for I had been holding my breath in awe the entire time. I relaxed and gently and slowly adjusted myself so that I was seated straight and at attention. I refused to bungle this most outrageous moment.

"Hello," I managed as I swallowed nervously. Upon my hello, I felt an energy that was as thick and as deep as the sea. I was surrounded by this powerful energy that emanated profusely from the serpent. It held me captivated. It punctured my heart, for I felt a thrust inward upon my chest. And then in a second I heard within myself the words, "Hello." This must have, no doubt, come from the serpent, for we were the only ones present. Not another soul could be seen for miles.

"How are you?" I did not know what to say.

I then heard, "As well and as sharp as ever."

I timidly giggled. "I am speaking to a serpent!" I exclaimed within my soul.

I gathered myself and said, "Might I ask you a few questions?"

"Indeed, you might."

"Are you the prodigy serpent that speaks the

language of the Gods?"

"That's what the humans of all the ages have called me, but I do not call myself that."

"What do you call yourself?"

"Not anything."

Realize that no words are being spoken; only feelings, sensations, images, and thoughts flashed upon me from, undeniably, the serpent.

"How is it that you can speak to the many? To me, even?"

"It is natural."

"I cannot do it," I said selfishly, for I prayed it would grant me the honor of its wisdom.

"All of those who inhabit the earth and beyond, whether they be human, animal, plant, or any of the others that are, as of yet, unknown, have the ability to communicate as I."

"Will you show me?" I said eagerly.

"There is nothing to show, for you are doing it as we speak."

"But I do not know what I am doing. You are the one doing it all, for without you I am afraid I would not be able to do what you insist I am doing."

"You can do whatever you desire to do, and you can do it without my presence. If you could not, you could not hear me."

I relaxed and said, "I have searched for you all these years and traversed high and low for you. I knew you were real."

"I am," agreed the serpent. As it slithered

nearer to me, it wormed its way around my neck and rested upon my shoulder. I felt its breath lightly caress my face. It was sweet and dewy. A very pleasant feeling, indeed. It comforted me as if it knew I needed some reassurance at that moment.

"So, if what I understand is correct, you are able to speak with all things, including humans, through images, feelings, and thoughts? This is what I gather from you because it is what I feel to be true in my heart and mind."

"Perfectly said by a human of this day, for they are the ones with the least understanding of what true language is."

"And what is true language?" I asked excitedly, for I was about to hear, to me, what was to be the most profound teachings I have ever been privy to.

"It is language that stands the test of time, that transcends all others, that has been here since before time and will be here after time; a language that can be understood by both beast and human, the plants and the trees, the moon and the stars, the visible and the invisible."

"I want to learn this language. It sounds glorious," I said, now in a dreamy state of ecstasy. "What shall I do?"

"Be still. Rid yourself of all in this world that brings you fear and heartache. Let go of all guilt, jealousy, fear, envy, shame, and hatred, and fill yourself with joy and appreciation. Be still and listen."

I sat with my eyes closed, listening intently to

its words, absorbing every flick and feeling, thought and image. I felt movement upon me. I opened my eyes, and to my disappointment, I found that the serpent had swiveled its way up the tree. "Wait!" I cried, but it continued on its way.

I resolved to take this knowledge with me and embrace it closely within my heart and mind, to study it, practice it, and nurture it. And as I strolled merrily, as if I had just found my first true love, I heard things that I had never heard before. I heard "Hellos" and "How-do-you-dos" and "Where are you off to" and "How pretty you are," and as I turned to see who these words sprang from, I saw birds, I saw trees, I saw plants, and I saw ants, bears, moose, and wolves. I was astounded, for I realized in that moment that I was communicating as the serpent. I could understand others besides my own. And then I heard a human. He spoke a language I was not familiar with, but somehow I could discern what he was saying. I felt his intentions, and when we greeted one another, we looked silently into each other's eyes. We smiled with a deep knowing and went our separate ways.

I picked up my pace and found myself skipping along, happier and with more clarity and understanding than I had ever had before, and thought to myself, "If you want to learn a language, choose a language that transcends all others, that embodies all there is, and that is fused with the most power; choose the language of the Gods."

Among Men

There once lived a stubborn old man who was set in his ways and knew what he knew to be true. He often traveled the woods with his grandson, impressing his knowledge upon the young lad.

As they trekked through the woods, they came across many an incident, and when they did, the grandfather would share his reasons for doing what he did. He would tell stories to the lad about bears and lions, wolves and eagles. Mostly, he boasted about how he conquered them with his sword. The boy, like any other, was impressed with his grandfather's conquests and began to mirror his words and actions in his day-to-day life, gradually becoming what his grandfather had become.

One day, while out in the woods, they came upon a serpent. Both reacted in kind. The grandfather drew his sword and pushed his grandson behind him protectively while the serpent stood up straight and faced the two and hissed. Now, there are snakes that would choose flight over fight, but this particular serpent chose fight.

"Stand back, son. I'll handle this vermin." Earlier, the grandfather had told the boy a story about how snakes were the spawn of the devil.

"Are you going to chop its head off, Grandfather?" the boy said eagerly.

"I plan to. Just stand back." And as the grandfather raised his sword to slash at the serpent's head, the serpent grew twenty feet tall. The grandfather stumbled back in horror and fell to the ground. The grandson followed and scurried behind the grandfather, their mouths agape.

The serpent hissed and slithered and flicked its tongue as it drew nearer to the humans, lowering its massive head to face what were now mere mortals quivering in their boots.

"How dare you raise your sword to me!" bellowed the serpent. "Who do you claim to be that you would threaten such a barbaric act?"

"You are the scum of the earth. You crawl around in secret, menacing the world. You're the devil on earth. You're a bad omen!" the grandfather hollered, though still in a frightful manner. He did not want to show any fear to his grandson.

"Why do you inflict these dishonorable words upon me?"

"Because that is what I know to be true."

"And how do you know this to be true?"

"From my father and his father before him, and I've seen it. I've witnessed it with my own eyes," the grandfather cried, though he did tell a fib, for the fact was that he had never seen, only heard.

"You are speaking from ignorance, for you do not know me nor can you claim intelligence in the matter of my kind. You sit and listen to stories of untruths and small, unworthy tales exaggerated beyond measure, and then you dare pass this ill will to a child so that he might continue the insanity of it all!" The serpent held fury in its eyes. The grandfather was nearly blinded by the sight of the serpent and covered his eyes. He wept.

"Grandfather?" yelled the boy, as he shook him. He stood up and turned to the serpent and shouted, "You can't hurt my grandfather!"

"Sit back!" hissed the serpent, smacking its tail upon the ground, thrusting the boy backward, atop his grandfather.

"You do not, as of yet, know what you say, for you are merely a mirror of your grandfather and not yet your own person. Silence from you is all I want to hear!" The serpent turned to the grandfather.

"Now, what shall I do with you?" it hissed manically. "Shall I constrict you within my coils and smother you, so you may no longer have the breath to spread your atrocities?" The serpent slowly twisted its way around the grandfather. "Or…"

"No, please don't!" interrupted the grandfather, with a trembling voice.

"No!" it said abruptly, releasing its grip on the grandfather dropping him to the ground. "I will not. Instead, I will do this." And the serpent lowered its head farther toward the ground and shoved its head through the bottom of the grandfather's foot. In hysterics, the grandfather screamed, "No, what are you doing?" He feverishly shook his leg but the serpent had already entered, now nearly past his knees. It swerved its way into the grandfather's groin, through his stomach, and as it squeezed its way through every inch of the old man's body, one could hear a pop, a spit, a boom, and a crackle. The grandfather moaned with each painful encounter, each release of an untruth, and ultimately ceased his resistance. He lay limp as the serpent continued its travels through his body, up his chest, and into each arm, his hands, and the tips of his fingers. Through his neck where his veins grew, it swerved, twisting itself within his face and bulging eyes, up his forehead till finally it squeezed its way out of the top of his head. The grandfather was near death with exhaustion.

The grandson lay over his body and said, "Grandfather, are you all right?" He was silent. "Grandfather?" The boy stared at his grandfather with awe, for right in front of his eyes, his grandfather began to slowly transform. No longer was he an ornery-looking old geezer, but instead he was a radiant young man whose skin glowed. His hair was as dark as the night sky, and his muscles were toned and sculpted.

"Awake," commanded the serpent.

The grandfather woke. He looked at his grandson. "Grandfather, you look like father!" The grandfather looked at his hands, touched his face. He grabbed his sword and looked at his reflection. He screamed with joy, shot up from the ground, and looked at the serpent.

"This is your work?" he said happily. "Why? Why did you do this for me? All these years I have traveled these woods in ignorance, I have done you and the likes of this grand forest wrong. I have judged you without knowing the truth. How can I repay you?"

"You shall go among men and teach the truth about my kind and those like us that have been defiled because of generations of ignorance. You shall rewrite what has been written. You shall tell new stories. You shall right what has been wronged. Take the boy and teach him properly. Do not spread hate and fear, but instead spread compassion and appreciation for all life."

"I will. I will. I promise you I will." The grandfather was beside himself, overwhelmed with joy and holding his grandson close to his heart.

"And remember this: if you at any time go back on your word, you shall return to the wretched old man you once were before your encounter with me."

"I promise you. I will not let you down."

And the grandfather and the boy left the company of the serpent and returned to their home. Upon their arrival, they set out to teach the truth about serpents. They went from town to town, village to village, telling stories of compassion, strength, understanding, and appreciation. These stories took hold in the consciousness of the masses, handed down from generation to generation, and soon abolished the stories of the old, making way for the beginning of a new era of appreciation for all life.

The serpent was pleased and returned to the woods.

To Be a Snake

Ah, to be a snake.

To slither here and there,
To and fro,
To swirl up a tree
And down below.

To twist and turn
Through the brush,
To take one's time,
Not to rush.

To bask in the sun,
To hide under a rock,
To wonder and ponder,
No matter a clock.

And then the time comes

To swerve in the mud,
Dig in with my snout,
Pushing and shoving
For the perfect workout.

Dark as the night,
Thick as the clouds,
All alone in my bliss,
Free of all crowds.

Slinking and winking,
Twirling and swirling,
Crawling and balling,
Whirling and curling,

Rubbing and scrubbing,
Scraping and draping,
Cracking and scratching,
Till I awaken.

Glimmering, shimmering,
About to come to
Glistening and whistling,
Happy and new.

THE SERPENT OF THE LAKE

Every year around springtime, the people who lived along the banks of a nameless lake gathered along the water's edge to watch the most spectacular event of the year. The children playfully ran toward the lake, laughing and giggling all the way until they finally seated themselves front and center. Following were the parents and elders of the community, with blankets and chairs, baskets of fruits and breads and meats and drinks, for this was sure to be an all-day event if one wanted it to be. The spectacle began in the wee hours of the morning and lasted to the wee hours of the night.

"Settle down," one woman said to her child, as the event was about to begin. Whispers and giggles could be heard while the crowd patiently waited, and then, out of the center of the lake, sprang a glorious silver-and-lime snake, straight up into the sky. "Ahhhh," cried the people, in wonder, and upon its descent and a splash through the water, they cheered.

Even the serpent angels of the heavens watched as their soulmate performed its seasonal dance.

"Does it not know?" said one of the angels, looking on in dismay.

"We think not," said another.

"Then maybe one of us should be so kind as to inform it."

"No, let it come to terms with it when it is ready," replied the wiser of the angels, so they continued to devote their hearts to their kin, along with the humans.

It leaped out of the waters
And into the air.
It twirled around
Without a care.

It dove in and out
In numerous strides,
To be seen and heard
Rather than hide.

It touched its lips
To its tail,
Creating a wheel
Along a trail.

It hissed and spit,
Tipped and danced,
Mesmerizing all
Into a trance.

The serpent continued its dance throughout the day and night. The crowds changed hands every few hours as some came and went to keep up with their chores and tend to their duties. The serpent angels who watched from above remained as well.

"I am not amused with this display," whispered the troubled serpent angel, and flew on its way to speak with the wind, the sun, and the land. Each was commanded to approach the serpent, whether it be alone or together. It was no matter as long as they confronted the serpent of the lake.

Still in its trance, the serpent continued its enchanting dance. The wind approached first and said, "My dear serpent, do you not know what has transpired in the past year?" blowing the serpent off course, but it was no bother to the serpent, as it proceeded in its work.

The sun approached second and said, "My dear serpent, do you not know what has transpired in the past year?" beaming its rays so intently as to blind the serpent, but no matter; the serpent carried on without a care in the world.

The land approached third and said, "My dear serpent, do you not know what has transpired in the past year?" trembling the waters in the hopes of derailing the serpent, but the serpent again paid no mind and persevered.

The wind, the sun, and the land returned to the serpent angel and said, "The serpent of the lake is stubborn and has not heard a word. It insists on continuing. There is nothing more we can do."

When all was quiet and the villagers returned to their homes, the serpent angel flew toward the serpent of the lake, appeared before it, and said, "My kindred spirit, do you not know what has transpired in the past year?"

The serpent stopped and faced the angel and said, "At last you have come for me."

"Then you are aware of what has transpired?"

"Yes, I am aware that I am the last of my kind."

"Then why have you persisted in your dance when you know no other will answer your call?"

"You have answered my call for spirit. I have enjoyed these last days expressing myself as a serpent, and it has been glorious, but now that you have heard my cries, I am ready to leave and start anew."

The serpent angel embraced the serpent of the lake, and together they danced its last dance for itself, its spirit, and its species.

They swirled and whirled,
Sneaked and peaked,
Slinked and blinked,
Rubbed their cheek.

Dove up and down,
Around the bend,
Never to return
Ever again.

The School Teacher

There once was an energetic and radiant young school teacher who lived in a small village, so small that it only had one school with one classroom with only ten children, one grocery store, one bank, and one street light that resided on the one street in the whole of the village, if you could even call it a street. She didn't mind at all, for small was all she knew.

One day she decided to take the school children for a trip into the small wooded area that surrounded the village. Though it was small, there were an array of unique animals that called these woods their home, like chipmunks and squirrels, mice and rabbits, raccoon and deer. But there was one animal in particular she wanted to introduce to the children, and that was her friend the serpent. She considered the serpent her friend because on occasion she would meander in the woods, and when she did she always happened upon the same serpent in the same place at the same time. She had grown so fond of the serpent that she shared her most intimate secrets with it, knowing that it would never dare tell a soul. She knew it understood every word she spoke, for when she did speak, it sat diligently and gazed upon her, not once leaving her sight.

"OK, children, gather around." The school teacher brought the children to the densest part of the woods and seated them in a semicircle around a half-moss-covered rock. The rock was lifted up on one end, forming a cave for a wandering critter seeking shelter.

Once the school children were settled down, the teacher walked over to the cave under the rock and whispered, "It's me. Are you in there?" She waited a moment and soon saw a little tongue flicking and sensing the air.

It inched its way out and stared the school teacher in the eye as if to say, "How can I help you?"

She said, "If you like, won't you please come out and show yourself to the children? I will keep you safe."

The serpent sensed the sincerity of the teacher and slowly inched its way out along the moss, peeking over the top of the rock. The children gasped with excitement as they spotted the deep black eyes of the serpent and a sliver of its head, for it had not completely shown itself. Their faces were as bright as the sun, and their mouths opened as wide as the ocean. They giggled and pointed and whispered to each other in awe.

"Now, children, settle down. This is my friend the serpent."

"Does he bite?" asked one youngster.

"No, he does not bite, but that's not to say that some snakes won't bite if they are frightened or happened upon without notice, so you must be cautious."

"He's pretty!" said another youngster, "Can we see all of him?"

"Pleeeeeeeeease!" chimed in all the other students.

"Let's ask. Mr. Serpent, can you show yourself fully, so that the children can see how beautiful you are?"

The serpent glanced around and flicked its tongue.

"He said yes," called out a student.

"And how do you know that?" asked the teacher.

"He told me. I heard him."

"You did?"

"Yup," said the student happily.

"Who else heard him?" asked the teacher, and nearly all the class raised their hands.

The serpent was delighted and felt safe with the children and knew that the teacher would keep it secure, so it crawled its way up the rock and coiled itself in the middle. The children smiled and said, "Can I touch him?" and another asked, "Can I feel his tongue on my cheek?" And with each question, the teacher said, "Let's ask." And they did.

Throughout the rest of the day, the children asked and the serpent answered, each respecting each other's boundaries. There wasn't any forcing or prodding or poking, nor was there any invasion of anyone's privacy. There was only a clear understanding and communication between the serpent and the children, animal and human, just like it ought to be, orchestrated by a thoughtful young school teacher with a big heart in a small village.

THE DARING FROG

A striking young autumn-colored snake happily lazed on an enormous lily pad fit for two, in the middle of a quaint pond in the forest. It soaked up the sun, relishing in powerful rays that warmed its entire body, from the tip of its nose to the edge of its long, slender tail.

While it lounged, in came hopping a lush emerald-green frog with protruding round eyes that were as dark as the night. It leaped atop the lily pad and began to croak and ribbit.

"What a daring little frog," thought the snake as it continued to doze.

"Ribbit, ribbit," exclaimed the frog.

The snake took no action upon the frog except to flick its tongue.

The daring frog and the loafing snake sat in accord for quite some time, but as the sun began to set, the snake became a bit irritated, perhaps a bit hungry. It slowly uncoiled its head, keeping it low and sharp, stalking the daring frog. It flicked its tongue, sensing its juiciness.

"Ribbit, ribbit!" said the daring frog, and as the snake struck, the frog leaped away by the skin of its webbed feet.

"Lucky frog," hissed the snake, and returned to its repose.

Alone

I want to be alone sometimes
To reflect upon myself,
Alone to think and ponder,
To get to know the world,

To listen to its whispers
And have it share with me
Its intentions, its reflections,
Its deeper mysteries.

I want to be alone sometimes
To understand the truth,
To hear the dirt beneath my skin
Tell me of its youth,

To receive a greater message
From the smiling sun,
To perceive its inner beauty
Till its time has come.

I want to be alone sometimes
To hear the silence in the air,
To feel the movement of my soul
Rejoicing in its fair,

For though I am a serpent,
I embody a kingly soul
Aware of its worthiness,
Aware of its final goal.

The Serpent, the Bear, and the Elephant

Once a serpent crawled along the banks of a raging river. As it slithered, it grew chilly and wanted to warm up so that it could continue on its journey. Where it was headed, it did not bother to wonder, for it was merrily following its heart to wherever it roamed. It was never one to worry about the future, for its focus was always in the present.

The serpent gazed up toward the sun and followed its rays to an enormous boulder that sat in the middle of the river. In the center of the boulder beamed a single ray that summoned it to a bath.

The serpent surmised from the looks of the river that it was flowing too wildly for it to swim across. It considered to its right and then to its left. There was no other way to cross. It then spotted a black bear across the river and flicked, "Excuse me, Mr. Black Bear; would you be so kind as to assist me across the river so that I might bask on that rock?"

The bear said, "What will you do for me in return?"

"I will give you my heartfelt appreciation and gratitude."

And the bear thought, and said, "Splendid."
The black bear dipped into the tumultuous waters of the river and was swept past the boulder and thus the serpent. He tried with all his might to swim against the current, but he tired, and while his strength weakened,

the river's strength grew with every effort. He glanced around for assistance and noticed an elephant lapping up the waters and said, "Excuse me, Mr. Elephant; would you be so kind as to carry me over to the serpent so that I might bring it to the boulder that is sitting in the middle of the river?"

And the elephant said, "What will you do for me in return?"

The black bear said, "I will give you my heartfelt appreciation and gratitude."

And the elephant thought, and said, "Splendid."

The elephant stepped into the water and trekked easily over to the black bear and scooped him up with his trunk. He carried the black bear over to the serpent, and the black bear leaned his huge head toward the serpent and said, "My dear serpent, crawl around my neck and hold on tight." The serpent did as it was instructed, and the elephant, with the black bear wrapped securely within his trunk and the serpent wrapped tightly around the head of the black bear, transported them to the boulder. The serpent crawled onto the rock and nestled itself comfortably in the center and began to soak up the sun's rays. Many thanks were exchanged between the serpent, the black bear, and the elephant.

"Now, my dear Mr. Elephant, would you be so kind as to bring me back to the other side of the river so that I might continue foraging for those delicious berries?"

"Surely," said the elephant, and he proceeded to transfer the black bear back to his side of the river. The elephant then returned to where he was stationed and lapped up the water, hurling it over his body.

Alone in the middle of the boulder that stood in the middle of the raging river, the serpent thought, "Ah, this feels good. Now, how am I going to disembark from this rock when the time comes? Not to worry, I will consider that later. For now, I will enjoy this moment." The serpent lowered its head and relaxed in the sun.

Forgive and Forget, Grudge and Remember

There once were two sets of two snakes; the first set called themselves Forgive and Forget, and the second set called themselves Grudge and Remember. Each pair set out to play the greatest game of all, the game of life. But they did not just want to live life, they wanted to live life well. They were born on the same day, within the same clutch of eggs, to the same mother, in the same environment. They traveled the same roads, encountered the same obstacles, and were endowed with the same tools.

The moment arrived when they set out on their own. On their life adventure, they traveled roads filled with many hurdles. They crawled about the earth with its branches and leaves and rocks and thorns and sticks and trees and bushes. One day they were each poked by the same stick and exclaimed, "Ouch!"

Forgive said gleefully, "I shall forgive."

Forget said happily, "And I shall forget."

Grudge said furiously, "I shall surely hold a grudge."

And Remember said angrily, "And I shall surely remember."

Forgive and Forget swiveled along with vigor and eagerness, while Grudge and Remember swerved with vengeance and disdain.

As they slithered about the earth they came to

a river crossing. They each sleeked in and were tossed about; taken for a wild ride down stream, bumping and thumping along the way.

Forgive yelled to his brother Forget cheerfully, "I shall forgiiiiiiiiive."

Forget replied playfully, "I shall forgeeeeeeet."

Grudge and Remember bellowed, irritated, "I shall surely hold a grudge," and, "I shall surely remember!"

The pairs of snakes finally caught hold of a branch and exited the water. Forgive and Forget slinked along fast and brightly. They held their heads high, looking out into the world for more adventure. Grudge and Remember creeped about nervously and distrusting, their heads low to the ground, wondering what displeasing adventure the world had in store for them next.

The group came across a few unsuspecting humans, who stepped on their tails. The snakes exclaimed, "Ouch!"

Forgive said, chipper and with a twirl, "I shall forgive."

Forget said, with a grin and a swirl, "And I shall forget."

Grudge shouted to Remember in disbelief, "I shall surely hold a grudge, my brother!"

Remember replied agreeably, "And I shall surely remember this debauchery!"

As they continued to play this game called life, the pairs of snakes no longer crawled together. Forgive and Forget swerved their way, and Grudge and Remember swiveled theirs, for, you see, they did not see eye to eye; hence, they were not the perfect match to traverse this land together.

They only rejoined when they happened upon the same rock years later. Forgive and Forget were as happy and cheerful as ever, feeling mighty spritely, twisting and whirling and twirling. Grudge and Remember were not so chipper. Their faces were drawn, their scales were bent and peeled, and they did not move as swiftly or as vibrantly. Their color was dull and muted, and they were not even going through a shed!

Forgive and Forget greeted their brothers Grudge and Remember and said with a smile, "My brothers, how are you faring?"

"Not so well," they chimed. "We are weary from life and are ready to crawl under this rock and die."

"But you mustn't," said Forgive and Forget.

"Why? Do you know of a better way to end this wretched life of ours?"

"Follow us," said Forgive.

And so the group slithered about the land together, and Grudge and Remember watched and learned from Forgive and Forget. Soon, they too began to forgive and forget, and when they did, they twirled about like newborn hatchlings. Their radiance returned, and they slithered with much stamina and vitality. Their skin rejuvenated and was brighter and glistened all the more.

Grudge and Remember turned to Forgive and

Forget and said, "I don't want to be Grudge," and, "I don't want to be Remember."

"What shall we call you?"

Grudge said, "I shall be called Love."

And Remember said, "I shall be called Laugh."

And so Forgive and Forget and Love and Laugh continued once again to crawl together in this game called life.

FRISKY

I'm feeling rather frisky;
I'm feeling rather sweet;
I'm feeling mighty naughty,
Eager to defeat.

Come, my little friend,
Right over here,
Right where I can see you,
Ripe to commandeer.

So plump and juicy,
Tasty and sweet,
What an aroma
Exuding from your feet.

Do not worry, dear;
It will end rather quick.
You won't feel a thing,
Not so much as a lick.

Steady, ready,
Stalking, gawking,
Adrenalin rising,
No more talking.

Strike!

Ahhh…

Frisky

Hollow, swallow,
Pushing down,
Resting securely
In my round.

Yum, Yum

Yum, yum,
Give it up.
Yum, yum,
Hurry up.

Yum, yum,
Fill my belly.
Yum, yum,
I am ready.

Yum, yum,
Not just one.
Yum, yum,
Give me two.

Yum, yum,
Don't be cheap.
Yum, yum,
Give me three.

Yum, yum,
You have more.
Yum, yum,
Give me four.

Yum, yum,
Don't be shy.
Yum, yum,
Give me five.

Yum, yum,
There you go.
Yum, yum,
Let it flow.

Yum, yum,
That was fun.
Yum, yum,
I am done!

THE SAVIOR

There once was a crab that lay in the sun, having itself a grand ole time by the shore. It gazed upon the ocean as its waves crashed in upon it. It dug in the sand to hide, poking its eyes out on occasion to witness the passersby, and proceeded to do what crabs do.

Then all of a sudden, it felt a harsh pull and a tug and was whisked away by one of its legs being thrown about in the air. It swung back and forth, to and fro.

"My golly," said the crab, "what has happened?"

It heard shouting and giggles and murmurs and slams and soon found itself atop a hard surface with big eyes staring and fingers poking.

"Look what I found!" yelled one.

"Oh, can we eat it?"

"How do you cook a crab?" asked another.

"You dunk it in hot, boiling water," said one.

"You pull its legs off," said another, as it dared.

The crab was beside itself and perplexed as to what to do, for its claws were rudely bound tight, affording it no chance to defend itself.

"Stop that!" A young girl dashed in. "You're hurting it!"

"No, I'm not. Crabs don't feel."

"Can you feel this?" And the girl yanked the boys arm, flailing his whole body about until he tumbled to the floor.

The boy screamed, "I'm telling!" And he ran off.

The girl grabbed the crab and brought it to her

room and untied its claws.

"There you go," she said softly. "That must feel better." The crab snapped its claws and sighed. "Yes, it does. Thank you for your kindness."

"You're welcome. I'm sorry about those horrid boys."

"No bother," said the crab.

"You are rather tasty, I must say. I've tasted one of you before. Not that I would do it again. I know you too well now." The girl blushed.

"Yes, we are rather succulent, to our misfortune. Would be much to our advantage if we were of a rancid flavor." The crab and the young girl lay on the floor, chatting away about this and that, when out from the corner crawled a taupe-colored snake. It slithered straight to the side of the young girl.

"How do you do?" It said to the crab.

"Better now, and you?"

"Rather well. I see you met the little girl."

"Yes, she is a savior."

All sorts of animals came sauntering into the middle of the girl's room from under the bed, in the closet, and cracks in walls: cockles, snails, shellfish, starfish, worms, and various creatures one would find by the different shores.

"She is indeed a savior," chorused the lot of them. "She looks out for all of us."

The little girl giggled.

"May I ask, little girl, are you going to cook me up or gawk at me through a jar or something quite unsuitable for a free-roaming animal such as myself?"

"No, I think not!" the little girl said with horror. "Everyone roams free here. You can leave whenever you like. You are not captive. Think of my room as a sanctuary should you find yourself in a quandary."

"Thank you. I am delighted." The crab smiled.

The snake interrupted with much curiosity. "My dear crab, under what circumstances do you find yourself here?" The other animals gathered around the crab and listened intently.

"It seems humans consider me rather tasty."

"Ah," said the snake. "Is it not better to be considered tasty by humans than frightening?"

And the crab said, "I suppose it does not matter much. Either way, you mustn't be faring very well if you find yourself at the mercy of a human."

"No, you mustn't," replied the snake.

All the animals, including the little girl, stared intently at one another in silence and then burst out laughing, for it is better to laugh than to cry.

MY DEAR HUMAN

I often wonder why my human worries about me so much. Does she not realize that I am a capable being, just as she, capable of making decisions for myself, capable of knowing what is good or bad for me, capable of knowing what harm might come my way if I trek certain parts of the house or if I decide to push my way through a hole? Does she not understand that I have awareness of myself, that I have awareness of her? Does she not understand that I can fend for myself, that I have desires that go beyond what she could ever imagine, though she is privy to some, for I have told her many? Does she not realize that I have my own will, that I am aware of the bigger picture, of hers and mine?

I wonder these things as she stares at me and I sense how she feels. Sometimes she's afraid of losing me to a horrific accident that she may cause unintentionally. Sometimes she's afraid of the lights burning too hot that they might cause a fire. Sometimes she wonders if I have all the comforts I need: am I warm enough or cool enough, is the air quality acceptable and clean, is my water clean? Is the dirt that I cozy moist enough?

Well, my human, I am aware, and I am all right. I am happy, but the one thing I don't understand and wish you would come to terms with is this new feeding pattern you have imposed upon me. You have told me many times that you fear me being overweight, yet I don't see it that way. I like to eat. My stomach craves food. I am craving as you write. I wish you would understand that I am healthy and that I do not worry about such things. I am concerned with what I am wanting at the moment, and what I want most of all is more food from you.

Dripping

There once was a serpent that dripped lazily from a tall, lanky tree in the rain forest. It swung by the tip of its tail, back and forth, back and forth. It enjoyed the cool breeze it created as it swayed, for it was unbearably hot and humid.

As the serpent swung so carelessly, it spotted a lone tiny droplet of water across the way on an adjacent tree. It was the only tree with humungous leaves that was blessed with one little dewdrop per leaf.

The serpent salivated at the sight of the droplet and drooled with anticipation of snatching it up with its tongue. "Juicy," it thought, "I'm going to swing and swing until I swing far enough to steal that droplet."

So the serpent swung and swung and pushed and pushed with all its might so that it would swing farther and farther. And as it swung, it neared the thirst-quenching droplet and flicked its tongue to catch it. "Drat!" it exclaimed. It missed.

The serpent lightly swung back and forth, taking a rest and surmising the situation, when upon glancing over at the lone droplet, it cried, "Oh my, the little dribble of water is falling. I must hurry before it falls to the ground." With much determination and focus, the serpent swung even harder than before, thrusting its swing with all its strength, and as it neared the droplet, it stretched out its tongue, and to its utter joy, the dewdrop fell, moistening and nourishing its palette. "Mm, satisfying," said the serpent, savoring the sweetness of the droplet. It swayed back and forth, back and forth, reveling in the droplet's juiciness, and upon satisfying its thirst, the serpent plummeted to the ground, for it swung so hard and so far and stretched so ferociously as to grab hold of the droplet that its tail unwound from the tree.

Bounce, bounce, bounce went the serpent on the ground. It felt rather dizzy in the head and stood still to regain its composure. Another serpent lay coiled beside it. It had watched its cousin serpent on its quest for the droplet and was quite fascinated with its unfolding.

It said, "My dear cousin, I have watched you from afar as you risked your very self for that little droplet. Might I ask, was it worth it?" Still a bit wobbly but appearing rather pleased with itself from the smile upon its face, the serpent flicked its tongue and answered, "Every bit of it."

THE PEARL

While writing with my human one day, we happened upon a sweet photo of a clam that sat on a white sandy beach with its mouth wide open and a perfectly round pearl seated in the center. She felt my enchantment with it as she closely observed me flicking my tongue. She noticed that when I am intense in the sensing of a thing, I flick my tongue rather quickly and very near to the object, akin to when humans study something they are fascinated with. They veer in really closely with their eyes or touch it softly with the tips of their fingers. She then asked me, "What is going on within you when you are sensing objects so intensely with your tongue?" This is what I said:

"When I move about, I flick my tongue to know where I am, what's in front of me, and where I am going; when I happen upon something that is intriguing, as the clam with the pearl inside, I zoom in on its essence and become much focused. I feel its energy, its shape, its size.

"I also know who it is, if it's safe, its beauty, its past, and its present.

"The sensation travels down into my body, and sometimes it makes me feel warm or cold and makes me aware of something within me. Different parts of my body are impressed upon. I may feel a twinge in my stomach or a stimulation of sorts in my bones or a particular bone.

"My tail may flutter; my heart may pound. With the clam with the pearl seated in the center, I felt warmth, beauty, serenity, and appreciation for its being, and once I am done, I move on, for I am on a mission to wherever it is I want to go."

IT DID NOT

It did not see itself as a nuisance but rather a necessary part of the whole.

It did not see itself as a pest but rather an intricate part of the environment in which it lived.

It did not see itself as less than but rather more than it appeared.

It did not want for anything but rather to be appreciated for its worth.

It did not want for praise but rather to experience its joy.

It did not fret over anything but rather was sure of who it was.

It did not wander aimlessly but rather knew exactly where it went.

It did not fear the unknown but rather was aware of all there is.

It did not pass any judgments but rather was focused on itself.

It Did Not

It did not compare itself to others but rather knew it was unique.

It did not see itself as a human but rather a serpent who dared to speak.

In Anticipation

In anticipation of what was to come, the serpent remained nestled within its home. It knew something great was happening outside. It saw within its mind the beauty and the splendor of what it was to receive once spring arrived. It saw the ins and outs and the ups and downs, the swerves and the curves. It felt the moistness, the dewiness, the roughness, the smoothness. It sensed the height and the depth, the weight and the gape, the diameter, parameter, and perimeter. It was tickled as it crawled in awe of it all. And it felt pleased that anyone would go to such great lengths to satisfy its desire to roam, to discover, to explore, to be independent, and to slither wherever it chose to, its desire to feel different textures against its skin that would stimulate it in its own unique ways. It was excited to traverse upon the natural substances of the world, though it resided in the home of a human. It was so delicious to imagine and anticipate and expect the best that its body jolted and kicked while it slept.

Soon, the day arrived and the door opened. The serpent was greeted with kisses and cuddled and set free to roam and discover its new play land.

It crawled and bawled.
It whirled and curled.
It glided and slinked
Upon the sink.

It moved and grooved
Along the wall.
It crept and sneaked,
Enjoying it all,

When it came upon something new.

It flicked and flicked
With great insight.
It found its play land
Pure delight.

The serpent investigated every crevice, every crack, every in and out, every up and down. It slithered over every hump and bump. It crawled into every hole and cave, testing its security, its fortitude. It glided through the moist grass and relished in the coziness it offered. It dug in the dirt and burrowed for a time. It emerged and climbed up a branch in a plant as the leaves softly grazed its skin. And then it returned to the cave that was set in the moist grass and slept comfortably, for all its expectations had been fulfilled. Never once did it doubt how magnificent its play land would be, and now it was time to enjoy it.

DANCE OF THE SERPENT

Two serpents, a male and a female,
One crawling from the east,
The other slithering from the west,
Searching for the perfect dance.

The male flicking its tongue,
Sensing the delicate fragrances of the female.
The female flicking its tongue,
Sensing the robust aroma of the male.

Each in a trance from the other,
They squirm and swivel with eagerness and anticipation.
Traversing through grassy lands, leaf-littered forests,
Over ancient rocks and thick branches, down the rough
bark of trees, in caves and under rocks.

Until they happen upon each other
In a shady spot under a grand old tree,
With the sun beaming through the leaves,
Resting upon their skin and glistening their eyes.

The male approaches, the female advances.
Face to face they flick their tongues.
The male lowers its head to the tail of the female.
He inches his way up, ever so slowly, as the female re-
mains erect.
He swerves around her,

Dance of the Serpent

Twisting himself tightly, binding her to him.
The female joins the dance and coils around the male,
binding him to her.

They meet eye to eye once more and sway back and
forth.
He dips below. She wiggles up.
She slides below. He rises up.
They lift their heads high, gazing upon the sky.

They twirl and swirl across the land,
Pressed upon one another,
Rustling the leaves, igniting the trees,
Enticing the birds and the bees.

The earth begins to rumble.
The clouds rush in!
The wind blows!
The trees sway!
The wolves howl!
The lions roar!
The elephants trumpet!
The birds sing!
The frogs croak!
The monkeys chatter!
The horses neigh!
The clouds rain!
The thunder booms!
The lightning strikes!
And the serpents rest…

THE RARITY

There once was a scientist and his colleague who often scoured the forest for new discoveries, whether it be a new species or the discovery of an unknown behavior or characteristic of an existing plant or animal.

Each morning they arose early and stuffed their backpacks and their pockets with an array of food, drink, and equipment: cameras, lights, sound equipment, measuring sticks, meters, water, savory snacks, and the like. They huddled together and decided what they would focus on for the day. Today, they chose to focus on sound.

With their sound equipment in hand, they eagerly headed out the front door and jumped in their Jeep. All the while, they proclaimed to each other, "This will be the day we discover something new!"

In the forest, they crisscrossed upon the fallen leaves, through the brush, over rocks and under trees, stopping here and there to zoom in close with their sound equipment on an unsuspecting critter minding its own business, most of the time startling the bugger and, to their chagrin, it scurrying off.

"Hear anything interesting?" asked the colleague.

"Not yet," answered the scientist.

Several hours passed, and suddenly the scientist gasped, with a smile upon his face.

"What is it?" asked the colleague excitedly.

"I hear a beautiful sound, like a humming.

Listen." He handed the headphones over.

"Oh my, that's lovely. Where is it coming from?"

"I don't know." The scientist put the headphones back on and pointed his equipment forward, backward, up and down, and side to side. As he could see it, there was no clear distinction as to where the sound was emanating from.

"Oh, it's so glorious. It sounds like a chorus. It's such a sweet sound. It's hard to describe. I don't want to stop listening," said the scientist, completely awestruck from its splendor. But in time the sound subsided.

The scientist and the colleague marked their location and headed back to camp. All night and into the wee hours of the morning, their conversation was filled with much joy and excitement about the sound they heard emanating from the forest.

Every morning for three weeks, they set out to the same area and heard the same enchanting melody without any clue as to where it was coming from. They pointed their sound equipment at trees and leaves, the bushes and grasses, the ants and the bees, the spiders and the praying mantis, the monkeys, and just about every creature they came in contact with until one day, they caught a break.

They stopped for lunch and the scientist gasped again. "There it is. It sounds very close; closer than before. It has got to be around here somewhere." And then he veered up and pointed his sound equipment, and for the first time, with his very own eyes, he saw what was humming the magical sound.

"My, gosh," the scientist whispered in awe, "there it is." The colleague peered up and rustled some leaves. "Be quiet," the scientist said. "We don't want to scare it."

"Oh my, it's gorgeous," said the colleague. "May I hear it?"

The scientist passed over the headphones.

"It's just so stunning. I would've never guessed."

While the colleague relished in the mystical melodies, she spotted the scientist inching his way closer to the creature.

"What are you doing?" she whispered.

"What else? I'm going to catch it and offer it to a zoo. We must breed it, dissect it, and study it to see how this phenomenon is possible."

"What? You can't do that. Leave it here where it belongs."

"Do you know what this creature, this rarity, is worth? Do you realize what this means to the science community? Never have I heard anything of the sort come from such a creature. This is unheard of!"

The colleague was beside herself. She took off the headphones.

"Leave it be. It belongs in the wild."

"It belongs in a zoo. It belongs to science to study. We can't deprive humanity of such a wonder. This is a tremendous discovery."

"We have the recording of its song. We can film it, and people can see it on their TVs. We can document it that way. There's no need to disrupt its life."

The scientist paid her no mind and continued his quiet ascent up the tree. The colleague yelled to the creature, "Run!"

"It doesn't understand you!" said the scientist, and as he neared closer to the creature, it lunged toward him with great velocity, striking him in the head. He plunged to the ground.

"Serves you right," said the colleague.

"Quick, get it!" said the scientist as he struggled to collect himself, but he was too dizzy. He looked up and cried, "It got away!" He slammed his fist against the ground.

"Good," whispered the colleague. As she glanced around, she spotted the rarity in the distance. She happily rested her eyes upon it as it eloquently slithered away.

CONCLUSION

Dumpling and I thoroughly enjoyed writing together. On a few occasions, I pushed myself on her to write when she clearly did not want to. Those stories came out subpar. As a result, five of them ended up on the cutting-room floor. There were also times when she was so focused on eating that all she could write about was food, as reflected in the poems *Frisky* and *Yum, Yum,* as well as showing a bit of frustration in *My Dear Human.* For your edification, since these writings I have changed her feeding pattern more to her liking.

This journey with Dumpling has surely brought us closer together. It might sound a bit strange, but since I have been consciously communicating with her, she has become more alive. She's like my sister. She clearly appreciates me as well, as shown in the poem *True Reflections.*

We had a grand time, and we hope it shows in the stories themselves. It was a unique experience and one that we will continue to delight in together.

***

In final conclusion, Dumpling wanted me to share the story below with you. It was written by her, Ivory, her sister mouse, and myself. One day I was sitting on the couch, and Dumpling wanted to write. I tried, but I couldn't. I told her my mind was preoccupied with Ivory, who had been sick. I vowed to invest my time only thinking of her in a good light in an attempt to assist her in healing. Then she said, "Why don't you invite Ivory in to write also?" I was so happy. What a great idea! And so this is the story that we wrote together:

Ivory the Great

There once was an adventurous little, white mouse with brilliant-red eyes named Ivory. She so enjoyed running and playing and discovering the world around her.

One day, Ivory came upon a towering mountain, but it fazed her not. She gladly climbed the formidable mountain, but she did not just climb, she dashed excitedly up till she arrived at its peak. Once there, she held her snout high and sniffed. She gazed down and felt big and proud, when all of a sudden, a mighty eagle snatched her up in its enormous talons. She held on tight as the eagle flew among the clouds and glided close to the canopy of the forest. She loved the feeling of flight. She loved looking out upon the vastness of it all. Her heart trembled with sheer joy. As they flew, without a moment's notice, the eagle unleashed its grip, and she tumbled down and down. She fell atop the leaf of a majestic tree, and she bounced and bounced and flipped and flopped.

"*Whoa!*" she exclaimed. "That was fun!" As she held on tight and did her utmost to balance herself on the wobbly leaf, she heard a grand voice say, "My dear Ivory, do not fret as you walk upon my leaves. With each step I shall offer you a steady, sure leaf."

"Thank you," she replied. "Will you be so kind as to create a blanket of leaves for me to cozy in while I gaze upon the sky?"

Without a word, the majestic tree began to gather its leaves together, forming a comfy blanket, as requested. Ivory lay down and snuggled within the nest of leaves. She relaxed from her long trek and adored all that surrounded her.

RIP Ivory – March 8, 2016

For other titles please visit:
http://www.nicolerivera.com

If you would like to book Nicole to read or speak at
your event, please e-mail:
cs@isaiahpublications.com

Thank you!